Owen the Oriole

A Chesapeake Bay Adventure

By Cindy Freland and Barbara Rew

Read with your heart

1

This book is dedicated to my beautiful daughters,
Andrea Bean and Alyssa Thomas.

Thanks for all the encouragement, love and laughter. I love you!

Cindy Freland

Book Acknowledgements

I'd like to thank my husband, Mark, for his love, encouragement, help and support. To my parents for instilling a love of reading and collecting books. To my niece, Anya, and her twins, Brenna and Collin, and my four nephews. To my G-d sons, Eddie and Robbie, and to Indya, I'm very proud of all of you. To the other "kids" I watched grow up, Chrissy and her brother, Marck, Aaron and Sara, Ben, Joanna and Matt, Gloria and Angie, thank you for letting me be a part of your life. To Paul Peterson for always having faith in me and to all my working kids of A Minor Consideration, http://aminorconsideration.org, I'll go on fighting the good fight as long as I am able. We will see National legislation in my lifetime. Barbara Rew

Order this book and other books written by Cindy Freland on www.Amazon.com and www.cbaykidsbooks.com.

Printed in the United States of America.

Paul Petersen

actor, singer, writer, child advocate
Gardena, California

Foreword

It isn't often that you get a chance to lend support to an important supporter of your life's work, but here we are. Barbara Rew has never lost sight of the child's soul. She cares about kids...especially those who are in difficult circumstances.

When you see the world through a child's eyes anything is possible, and here in the wilds of the Chesapeake Bay, the possible becomes real. You'll enjoy this whimsical effort. Suspend disbelief and take wing.

The little chick wiggled, wriggled, and pecked, and wiggled some more. Then he heard a crack. He kept pecking until he saw light, it hurt his eyes a little but somehow he knew he was doing the right thing. Finally he had pecked enough that he was free of the egg.

The first thing he heard was a very small voice saying "hello."

"What be you on my top," the little chick asked?

"I'm Beverly the Butterfly," Beverly answered.

"A flutterby?" the little chick asked.

"That will do for now," she answered.

"Why you be on my top?" he asked.

"You're just hatched and are all wet and I don't want to get my wings wet. Besides, you're just a chick and you don't know enough not to eat me or at least try and taste me," she said.

"Oh," was all the little chick could warble. He made note that he didn't eat flutterbys.

Then he asked, "If you're a flutterby, what am I?"

"You're a bird, an Oriole," his father told him. "A hungry little bird at that," then his father gave him a bit of cherry to eat. The little chick liked that and chirped for more.

"Father Oriole I'm going to the next nest over to tell them one of your eggs hatched. What name you have given him?" Beverly asked.

"His mother and I have named him Owen," Father Oriole told her.

"Owen the Oriole is a good name for him," Beverly said and smiled at Owen as she flew off.

Owen woke from his nap to find he had a new brother, Olaf, and sister, Odessa, who had hatched from their eggs. Being that he was first hatched he decided to share some of what he had learned.

"We are birds and we don't eat flutterbys," Owen told Olaf and Odessa proudly.

"That's right, you don't eat butterflies," Beverly said as she landed on Owen's head.

"This is Beverly, she's my first best friend," Owen told Olaf and Odessa.

Owen was six days old when he saw his first dragon human. It was just like his mother had told him. The human ate a fire stick and then breathed smoke. Both his parents had warned him to stay away from dragon humans and their very dangerous fire sticks.

His mother had told him about the coverings that humans wear to conceal their scales. He saw for himself they left hot fire sticks on the ground. His parents always worried when they were hopping around on the ground that one of the fire sticks would blow in their direction and burn their feet. It was a constant worry for most animals that live near Owen's nest. His neighbors were always happy when high tide came. The water would wash over the ground and if there was a hot fire stick the water would wash it away.

His father had explained that things left on the ground, including fire sticks, bottle caps, and newspaper, are trash. They are dangerous and need to be placed into a trash can. He had heard

that animals had swallowed trash and were sick or they got trash stuck around their necks.

Their father brought worms, bugs, and berries to eat from the nearby farms. Their favorite things to eat were tent caterpillars. Their dad beat the caterpillar against a branch to scrape off the protective hairs before allowing Olaf and Odessa to eat it.

As Owen grew, his orange and black colors became more noticeable. He got more and more curious about the world around him. He watched children coming to school and going home. He watched the farmers planting their spring crops, including broccoli, cabbage, potatoes, cantaloupe, and watermelon. He also

watched the mothers planting their flower gardens with marigolds, petunias, and zinnias.

But he often wondered what else was out there. What else could he see and do? His parents told him that he was special because he was first to hatch and was the smallest in the family. But what made him so special?

One warm day in April, Owen watched a few of his friends skateboarding on a plastic bottle cap. They would carry the cap to the top of the roof of a house, jump on the bottle cap, and ride it down the roof. Owen tried it and he had great fun. Owen knew the

bottle cap was trash so he put it into the trash can when he was finished with it.

Owen liked to sharpen his beak by scraping it on a stone wall at the farm. After it was sharp enough, Owen would poke his beak into the darkest, ripest blackberries and use his tongue to suck the juice. In summer, he ate all the fruits he could so he would have energy to migrate to Mexico in the fall.

Eight year old Mark was whistling his favorite tune. All of a sudden he heard his whistle repeated. He wondered where that sound could have come from. He looked around and saw a bird nest on the top branch of a tall maple tree. The smallest bird was

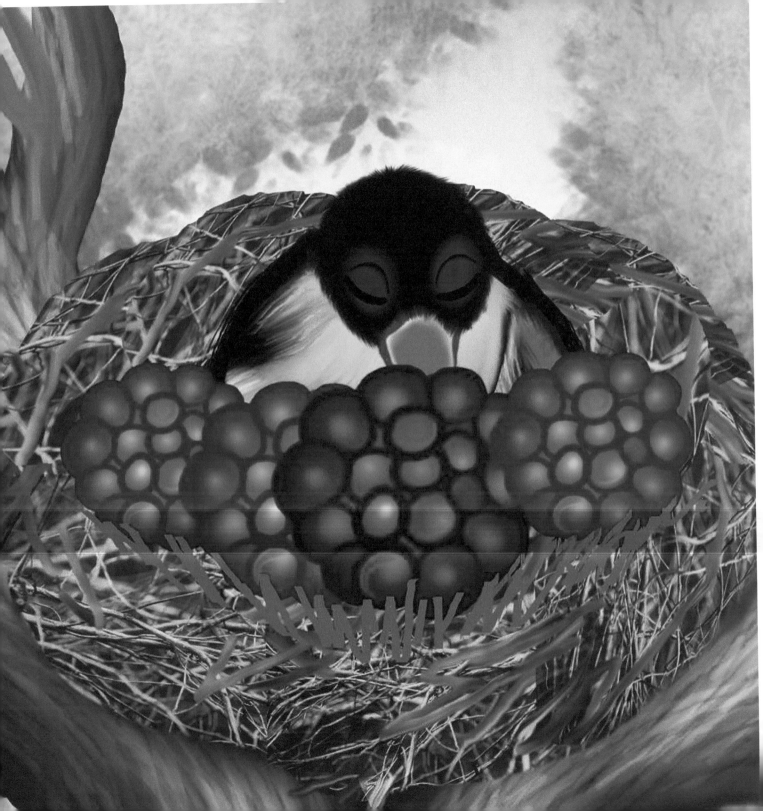

repeating Mark's whistle. Mark smiled as he looked at the bird and he turned to walk in the school door.

Owen noticed that school children were gathering in the field. The teacher was holding a large, white "egg" in one hand and wearing a cover on his other hand. The children were standing all around the field ready to play the game. The teacher threw the "egg" to Mark. Mark hit the "egg" with a stick and it flew across the field.

"What are they doing? They will crack that "egg" by hitting it like that. I need to do something to save it!" said Owen.

Owen was determined to save that "egg." So he flew over to his friend, Sebastian the Squirrel, and asked for his help.

"Sebastian, could you please help me? I want to try to save that "egg" and maybe we could... yes, see that newspaper over there? Maybe you could help me put the "egg" on it and I could carry it to my nest," asked Owen.

Sebastian and Owen tried and tried but the "egg" ripped through the wet newspaper.

"Thanks for trying Sebastian. We have to try another way to save that "egg." But trash belongs in the trash can so let's put the newspaper where it belongs," said Owen.

A few members of the Chestertown Cheetah's were asked to put the equipment away after ball practice. The children were tossing the ball and the ball slid down a storm drain beyond their reach. The children talked about the cost of replacing the ball and how much it might cost them their allowances.

Owen was watching from the sky and wanted to help. He noticed Chester the Chipmunk below and flew down to ask for his help.

"Chester, could you please help me? I want to try to save that "egg" and maybe we could... yes, you're small enough, could you please push the "egg" out of the storm drain?" asked Owen.

Chester pushed the "egg" and hid it under some leaves until Owen could figure out a way to get it to the nest.

A human dragon was out by the storm drain smoking a fire stick and kicked at the leaves to put it out and found the "egg." He returned the ball to the boys and Owen was very unhappy to see this. Owen knew the fire stick was trash so he put it into the trash can.

The children were ready to play the final game of the season. The opposing team hit the ball into the outfield where no player was stationed.

Owen walked around under the bench and thought, "how can I pick up this "egg?"

He stepped into some sticky gum that a child had left on the ground. The gum stuck to Owen's feet.

Owen got an idea, "what if I stick the "egg" to the gum? Maybe I can save the "egg."

The ball fell off. Owen tried to stick the ball to the gum again. After several tries, he realized the gum is too dry and it was not sticky enough to stick to the ball. How could he make the gum sticky again?

Many people were sitting on the benches watching the children play the game. Owen watched the people eat hot dogs. Some were eating popcorn and peanuts. Some were drinking sodas. Owen saw a child drip some soda on the bench and the boy got his hand stuck on it. So Owen thought the soda might help make the gum sticky again.

Owen picked up the gum in his beak and accidentally swallowed it. UGH! He felt sick. Owen picked up another piece of gum with one foot and carried it over to the soda drip on the bench. The gum soaked up the soda and Owen carried it back to the ball. The ball stuck to the sticky gum again and he was able to carry the ball a longer distance. Owen was right!

Owen got as far as home plate when he dropped the "egg." The umpires argued about Owen's "help" but in the end, the runner on the opposing team was out and the Cheetah's won the game.

The Cheetahs were laughing and cheering. Owen had helped them win the final game of the season. He didn't know why they were

happy as he watched the "egg" roll under a bush. Owen finally saved that "egg!"

The boys and girls of the team left a pile of cherries bigger than Owen to thank him for his help winning the baseball game.

Maryland History and Heritage

Maryland is a Mid-Atlantic state that's defined by its abundant waterways and coastlines on the Chesapeake Bay and Atlantic Ocean. Its largest city, Baltimore, has a long history as a major seaport.

The state inhabits a great number of white-tailed deer, especially in the woody and mountainous west of the state, and overpopulation can become a problem. There is a population of rare wild horses found on Assateague Island. Maryland's reptile and amphibian population includes the diamondback terrapin turtle, which was adopted as the mascot of University of Maryland.

Maryland joined with neighboring states during the end of the 20th century to improve the health of the Chesapeake Bay. The bay's aquatic life and seafood industry have been threatened by development and by fertilizer and livestock waste entering the bay.

Chestertown Tea Party

The **Chestertown Tea Party** was a protest against British excise taxes which, took place in May 1774 in Chestertown, Maryland. Chestertown tradition says that, following the example of the famous Boston Tea Party, colonial patriots forcibly boarded the ship *Geddes* in daylight and threw its tea cargo into the Chester River.

When news of the closing of the port of Boston reached the Chesapeake Bay port of Chestertown in the spring of 1774, town leaders had a meeting to discuss the necessary actions. The local chapter of the Sons of Liberty wrote a list of grievances, which became known as the "Chestertown Resolves." These stated that it was unlawful to buy, sell, or drink tea shipped from England.

The celebration is each Memorial Day weekend in Chestertown, Maryland with a festival and historic reenactment called the Chestertown Tea Party Festival. Check out the website at www.chestertownteaparty.org.

Becoming a State

After the war, Maryland ratified the new United States Constitution and was the seventh state to join the Union on April 28, 1788.

War of 1812

Maryland was also involved in the War of 1812 between the United States and Great Britain. Two major battles occurred. The first was a defeat in which the British captured Washington D.C.

in the Battle of Bladensburg. The other was a victory where the British fleet was held off from capturing Baltimore. It was during this battle, when the British were bombarding Fort McHenry, that Francis Scott Key wrote *The Star-Spangled Banner* which later became the national anthem.

America in Miniature

Maryland possesses a variety of landscapes within its borders, contributing to its nickname *America in Miniature*. It ranges from sandy dunes loaded with seagrass in the east, to low marshlands teeming with wildlife and large bald cypress trees near the Chesapeake Bay, to gently rolling hills of oak forests in the Piedmont Region, and **pine trees** in the mountains of Western Maryland.

PLEASE HELP THE CHESAPEAKE BAY

The Chesapeake Bay is a gorgeous place to live, work and play. Check the website at www.cbf.org for more information on what you can do to help.

What can you do to help?

1. Become a member of the Chesapeake Bay Foundation and other Bay organizations.
2. Volunteer to help clean the Bay.
3. Join the Chesapeake Bay Action Network and speak out for the Bay!
4. Check the education section if you are a teacher. There are professional development initiatives, student education programs and more.
5. Throw trash in trash cans or take it with you.
6. Never throw anything into the Bay.
7. Never harm animals or dig up plants.
8. Help spread the word about the Bay.
9. Swim and fish in designated areas.

MORE BOOKS WRITTEN BY CINDY FRELAND

You will find books written by Cindy Freland on Amazon.com and cbaykidsbooks.com:

Jordan the Jellyfish: A Chesapeake Bay Adventure
Curtis the Crab: A Chesapeake Bay Adventure
Heather the Honey Bee: A Chesapeake Bay Adventure
Oakley the Oyster: A Chesapeake Bay Adventure
Olivia the Osprey: A Chesapeake Bay Adventure
Lila the Ladybug: A Deep Creek Lake Adventure
Vandi the Garden Fairy
Christmas with Marco: A Chesapeake Bay Adventure
Chester the Chipmunk: A Chesapeake Bay Adventure
Paisley the Pony: An Assateague Island Adventure
Macy the Mermaid: A Chesapeake Bay Adventure

Author:
Cindy Freland

Cindy Freland's inspiration comes from her love of children and animals. Most of her children's books are based on true events. Her passion is teaching children about the beauty and the bounty of the Chesapeake Bay. She started a children's book series about the bay in 2013. You can find her books on www.amazon.com and on www.cbaykidsbooks.com. Freland founded Maryland Secretarial Services, Inc. in 1997 and lives in Bowie, Maryland.

Author:

Barbara Rew

Barbara K. Rew has been a child advocate for most of her adult life. Currently she is the Senior Vice President of Legislative Affairs for A Minor Consideration. Ms. Rew feels she owes a debt to children working in the entertainment industry, because as a sick kid she watched a lot of television. "I feel these people gave up their childhoods to entertain me," she says. Since 1993, as a member of A Minor Consideration, Ms. Rew served on a number of committees and boards dealing with non-profit groups and Government agencies. She is also the Special Program Coordinator for The Entertainment Industries Council.

She hosted a community cable access television talk show, Barbara's Choice Personalities, where she interviewed many people from the community and throughout the nation involved with children's issues. including A Minor Consideration's founder and president emeritus Paul Petersen.

Ms. Rew's other community activities include serving as a fundraising speaker for the Hospital for Sick Children. Her efforts assisted the hospital in obtaining the funds for building a new wing and garage. She was a member of the Friends of the Bowie Library bringing her love of reading to children. "One of my proudest days as a child was when I got my first library card. I want all children to feel the pride and joy I felt from using the public library." Her efforts supported the funding and building of Opportunity Park, the first park to be fully accessible for all children including children with disabilities. She also supports several volunteer groups for children, women, disabled people and the elderly. Ms. Rew also served as a volunteer on the Bowie Hotline in the late 1980's and in the 1990s she supported raising funds for Bowie's Center for the Performing Arts.

Ms. Rew has been an employee for the federal government for the past 35 years. Some of the activities she enjoys are reading biographies, cooking, and travel.

This is Ms. Rew's first children's book. https://www.facebook.com/Rewbarb-Productions-728621384158813/

Illustrator: Emily Hercock

I am a freelance illustrator based in a small village in Norfolk, UK and have illustrated over 20 books in my three-year career. I work from my home where I live with my wonderful husband and Dougal, my cat, who keeps me company as I work.

I began drawing as soon as I could hold a pen and now at age 26 I am proud to run my own business, "Emily's illustrations," doing what I love as a career.

I left school at age 17 with top grades in GCSE art but was unable to go on to further education due to family circumstances. I went straight to work at various retail stores where I would always be doodling on the back of receipts!

I was married in 2014 to my husband, Michael Hercock, who has supported me in starting and growing my business. I doubt I would be where I am now without his encouragement and belief in me and my work.

I became ill in 2015 with Chronic Fatigue Syndrome and had to give up working as a cleaner. I was determined to continue to work and whilst scrolling through a chat room for authors (where I was looking for advice on a book I was trying to write) I found a lady looking for an illustrator. I applied and that was the beginning of my career.

Now in year four of my career in illustration and I have had the privilege to work with Cindy Freland and her wonderful series of children's books about the Chesapeake Bay area. Illustrating her book "Paisley the Pony" and "Macy the Mermaid" have been nothing short of a delight.

My business continues to grow and I continue to love illustrating for the world's children.

You can find my website at: http: www.emily-jade-illustrator.com.

CPSIA information can be obtained
at www.ICGtesting.com
Printed in the USA
BVHW020858291018
530935BV00024B/14/P